SUPERHERO SCHOOL

Thunderbot's Day of Doom

Also by Alan MacDonald

The Superhero School series:
The Revenge of the Green Meanie
Alien Attack!
Curse of the Evil Custard

The Troll Trouble series:
Trolls Go Home!
Trolls United
Trolls On Hols
Goat Pie

The History of Warts series:
Custardly Wart: Pirate (third class)
Ditherus Wart: (accidental) Gladiator
Honesty Wart: Witch Hunter!
Sir Bigwart: Knight of the Wonky Table

The Iggy the Urk series:
Oi, Caveboy!
Arrrrgh! Slimosaur!
Euuugh! Eyeball Stew!
BOOOM!

SUPERHERO SCHOOL

Thunderbot's Day of Doom

Alan MacDonald

Illustrated by Nigel Baines

BLOOMSBURY
LONDON OXFORD NEW YORK NEW DELHI SYDNEY

Bloomsbury Publishing, London, Oxford, New York, New Delhi and Sydney

First published in Great Britain in January 2016 by Bloomsbury Publishing Plc
50 Bedford Square, London WC1B 3DP

www.bloomsbury.com

A CIP catalogue record for this book is available from the British Library

ISBN 978 1 4088 2526 6

MIX
Paper from
responsible sources
FSC® C020471

Printed and bound in Great Britain by CPI Group (UK) Ltd, Croydon CRO 4YY

1 3 5 7 9 10 8 6 4 2

MEET THE SUPERHEROES OF MIGHTY HIGH...

DANGERBOY (aka Stan)

SPECIAL POWERS: Radar ears that sense danger

WEAPON OF CHOICE: Tiddlywinks

STRENGTHS: Survival against the odds

WEAKNESSES: Never stops worrying

SUPER RATING: 53

FRISBEE KID (aka Minnie)

SPECIAL POWERS: Deadly aim

WEAPON OF CHOICE: 'Frisbee anyone?'

STRENGTHS: Organised, bossy

WEAKNESSES: See above

SUPER RATING: 56

BRAINIAC (aka Miles)

SPECIAL POWERS: Super brainbox
WEAPON OF CHOICE: Quiz questions
STRENGTHS: Um . . .
WEAKNESSES: Hates to fight
SUPER RATING: 41.3

PUDDING THE WONDERDOG

SPECIAL POWERS: Sniffing out treats
WEAPON OF CHOICE: Licking and slobbering
STRENGTHS: Obedience
WEAKNESSES: World-class wimp
SUPER RATING: 2

HE THOUGHT ABOUT NOTHING ELSE

EVERY DAY HE PRACTISED HIS WEATHER FORECAST!

Dennis gave the weather rain or shine, until one day...

50p

FREE DONUT INSIDE!

THE DAILY GRIME

IS THIS THE MOST BORING MAN ON TV?

He has been in living rooms s us to sleep for Dennis Trigg the most bor on TV? Doe you the win be make yo it's always even in the

Chapter 1
Weird Science

At Mighty High it was the summer term and the students were busy at work in the science lab. Among them were Stan, Miles, Minnie and Pudding the Wonderdog, the four members of

the Invincibles.

Every year the Dame Dorothy Wingnut Prize for Science was presented to the pupil who came up with the most original scientific invention.

In any ordinary school this might have resulted in a glut of pencil sharpeners or novelty lunch boxes, but this was Mighty High – the school for young superheroes – so the gadgets were of a different order altogether. Stan's classmates were working on fireproof capes, silent shoes and hamster-tracking devices. Stan had never won a science prize – in fact, he'd never won anything unless you counted a goldfish at the fair.

'There,' he said, tightening a screw and trying on his invention. 'What do you think?'

Pudding cocked his head on one side. Minnie frowned.

'A pair of glasses,' she said. 'What's original about that?'

'Ah,' said Stan. 'But say you're wearing your glasses and it starts to rain.'

'I don't wear glasses,' objected Minnie.

'Yes, but say you did,' Stan continued. 'Then all you have to do is press this tiny button and ...'

Minnie rolled her eyes. 'Seriously?' she said. 'Glasses with windscreen wipers?'

'Brilliant, eh?' said Stan. 'Perfect for flying in the rain. And check this out, they've got two speeds: fast and superfast.'

He pushed the button again and the tiny wipers zipped back and forth in a blur of speed. Stan turned them off.

'Clever AND original,' he said modestly. 'Especially if you happen to wear glasses.'

'Which I don't,' repeated Minnie. 'How many superheroes can you name who wear glasses?'

'Well, Miles, for one,' said Stan. 'He's not a superhero yet but he will be one day. Where's he gone, anyway?'

They found Miles in another corner of the science lab, putting the finishing touches to a pair of gloves. They looked like fairly ordinary gloves except that they were made of unusual shiny material that glittered like frost.

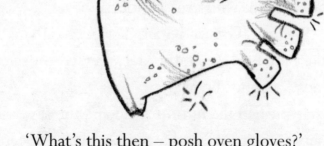

'What's this then – posh oven gloves?' asked Stan.

'Very funny,' said Miles. 'Try them on.'

Stan did as he was asked.

'How do they feel?' asked Miles.

'A bit too big,' said Stan. 'They're not exactly super-stylish, are they?'

'That's not the point,' said Miles. 'It's what they do that counts.'

'What do they do?' asked Minnie.

'They're magnetic,' Miles informed them. 'I call them Mega Gloves. There are a million magnetic microfibres in there so tiny that they're invisible to the naked eye.'

Stan raised his eyebrows. Miles's superhero name was Brainiac but even so, this sounded a bit far-fetched. Stan wiggled his fingers.

'So, how do they work?' he asked.

Suddenly, something shot off a desk and attached itself to the Mega Gloves. It was a paper clip. A moment later it was joined by a screwdriver, a pair of scissors and the name tag from Pudding's collar. In a few seconds the Mega Gloves were covered in metal objects.

'You're not kidding!' gasped Minnie. 'They are magnetic!'

'Of course they are,' said Miles. 'Say someone's pointing a laser gun. You could disarm them.'

'Magnetic gloves?' sneered a voice. 'How original!'

They all turned to see Norris Trimble, wearing his thick glasses and usual smug expression. Norris was probably the weediest boy in the school. He came over dizzy if he stood on a chair. On the other hand he was a science genius who wore his own white coat to lessons. For weeks Norris had been staying behind after school to work on some kind of secret project.

Miles glared at him. 'What's it got to do with you, Norris?' he demanded.

'I just wouldn't want you to waste your time,' said Norris. 'You're hardly going to win with a pair of oven gloves.'

'Mega Gloves,' corrected Miles.

'Whatever,' said Norris.

'And what's your brilliant invention, Norris?' asked Minnie.

Norris tapped his nose. 'Ah, that would be telling,' he smirked. 'Wait until tomorrow when they announce who's won!'

They watched him go. Stan sighed. 'He can be really annoying sometimes,' he said.

'What do you mean sometimes?' asked Miles.

They were interrupted by the arrival of
their head teacher. Miss Marbles clapped her
hands to get their attention.

'Now, as you know, tomorrow we're
holding the Science Awards,' she said. 'We shall
be selecting three finalists who will compete
for the award. And this year I'm delighted to
say we have a very special guest to present the
prize – a celebrity, in fact!'

A buzz of excitement ran round the room.

Who did Miss Marbles have in mind? Maybe it was a famous footballer or a glamorous film star? Stan wondered if it could even be Captain Courageous, probably the most famous superhero on the planet and the face of Titan Shampoo for Men.

Miss Marbles waited for quiet.

'You're very lucky that our Science Prize will be presented this year … by Dennis Trigg.'

Dennis Trigg? Stan and his friends looked at each other, mystified.

'You know, Dennis Trigg! He used to do the weather forecast on TV,' said Miss Marbles.

Stan rolled his eyes. A weatherman? He'd been expecting someone who was actually famous. Stan never understood why his parents watched the weather forecast every night without fail. It had to be the most boring programme on television!

Miss Marbles had pulled down a screen and was showing them a TV clip she'd found on the internet. A man in a grey suit and tie was reading the weather forecast in a voice that was duller than a cloudy day in Cleethorpes.

… And tomorrow another dry day with a few fog patches which will clear away during the morning …

Miss Marbles zapped off the TV screen and turned back to the class.

'There you are – Dennis Trigg!' she said.

But no one was listening because they were all slumped face down on their desks.

DON'T BE GOOD, BE SUPER.

PROPERTY OF
MIGHTY HIGH SCHOOL

The Pocket Guide for Superheroes

Everything you need to know
to save the world.

2
GADGETS, GIZMOS AND GLITCHES

In days gone by, a superhero arrived on the scene armed only with brute strength, quick reactions and limited intelligence. But times have changed. These days, crime fighters often have more gadgets than a space station.

Here are a few examples from the gallery of gizmos:

1. HOVER BOOTS

Because why walk when you can make like a hovercraft.

2. INFLATISUIT

Are you small, skinny or weedy? Do villians kick sand in your face? No problem — just inflate this suit for instant superhero muscles.

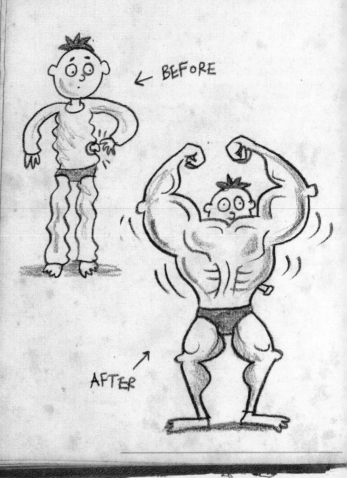

← BEFORE

AFTER →

3. UTILITY BELT

For those pesky missions when you don't know what to expect.

GAS MASK

PENKNIFE

SPARE PANTS

RAIN CAPE

SUPER SNACKS

4. SMOKESCREEN CHEWING GUM

In a tight corner? Smokescreen gum covers any sticky situation.

5. DEATH STARE GLASSES

With these specs, no one will call you four eyes ever again.

Chapter 3
Roboflop

Stan sat in the school hall, fiddling with his rainproof glasses. The judges – Miss Marbles, Professor Bird and Miss Stitch – had already made their inspection of the children's projects and now the head teacher was about to announce the names of the three finalists.

Stan had a feeling his chances of winning were slim. Miss Marbles' verdict on his invention had been something like 'Hmm, very nice, Stanley', which hardly qualified as wild enthusiasm.

Minnie's Xtra-Stretch Dog Lead had caught Miss Stitch's attention, but she had pointed out that it was aimed more at dog owners than superheroes.

Miss Marbles came on stage along with a man wearing a baggy grey suit and a terrible tie. Stan recognised him as Dennis Trigg, the former weatherman and special guest. He didn't look like a man who was mobbed by

autograph hunters
everywhere he went.

Miss Marbles
searched for her
reading glasses and
located them on her
head. She smiled.
'Well, the judges have
been tremendously
impressed by the
sheer variety of your
ideas,' she said. 'But
we have to find a
winner, so we've

narrowed it down to our three finalists who
now have a chance to show us their projects.
So, the first up is Tabitha Spinks.'

Tabitha Spinks, a girl with wild curly hair,
bounded on to the stage.

'My invention is the Exploding Pencil,' she
announced.

Miles rolled his eyes, but Stan sat forward. This ought to be worth watching.

'You can use my pencil in any situation,' Tabitha explained. 'If you need to escape by blowing a hole in a wall for instance. All you do is press the button on the end like this, then stand well back and wait.'

She set the pencil down and quickly withdrew to the side. Miss Marbles and the others on stage crouched down, plugging their fingers in their ears. Tabitha began a countdown as her schoolmates joined in …

'FIVE, FOUR, THREE, TWO, ONE … !'

Nothing.

'Oh,' said Tabitha. 'Um.'

Miss Marbles came forward cautiously. 'Thank you, Tabitha, it's a lovely idea, but perhaps it needs a little more work,' she said. Slightly crestfallen, Tabitha pocketed the pencil and was about to leave the stage when …

The audience burst into applause.

Stan noticed that Dennis Trigg was looking rather baffled. No one had explained to him that Mighty High was a school for junior superheroes. He was probably wondering why the pupils were allowed to experiment with exploding pencils.

Miss Marbles moved on quickly. 'So, let's welcome our next finalist. Where is Miles?'

Miles blinked in surprise. Stan thumped him on the back.

'Wish me luck,' muttered Miles.

He climbed on to the stage and went to the microphone.

'This is my science project. They're called Mega Gloves,' he told the audience, holding them up. 'They may look like ordinary gloves but in fact they contain millions of magnetic microfibres …'

His audience looked impressed, mainly because they had no idea what he was talking about.

'Maybe it's best if I show you,' said Miles. 'Imagine I'm locked in a locked room and the key is out of reach.' He placed a key on the small table beside Dennis Trigg and took a few steps back.

Wearing the Mega Gloves he stretched out his hands. Immediately the key zipped across the stage and shot into his hand.

Unfortunately Miles hadn't considered that there might be other metal objects on the stage – Miss Marbles' glasses, the Science Award Trophy and the buckle on Dennis Trigg's belt, to name a few. All of these things obeyed the pull of Miles's magnetic gloves and zoomed into his hands.

There was an awkward silence as Miles returned the objects to their owners. As he left the stage, only Stan and Minnie clapped.

'Well, that went well,' said Stan as Miles sat down.

'It just needs a few adjustments,' muttered Miles. 'The magnetism is more powerful than I thought.'

There was one last finalist to come and to nobody's real surprise it was Norris Trimble. He took to the stage, wearing his white lab coat and protective goggles, which made him look even more like a mad professor than usual. His science project was draped in a white sheet.

'OK, listen up, peabrains,' he said. 'I'll try to make this easy for you to understand. My invention is called … ALBOT!' He whipped off the white sheet.

Dennis Trigg suddenly sat forward, paying attention. He certainly hadn't expected a robot.

Norris switched it on and the robot clicked
and whirred, swivelling his head to face the
audience. Norris smiled.

'Ask him a question,' he said.

'Very well,' said Miss Marbles. 'What's the name of my cat?'

Norris rolled his eyes.

'I meant a scientific question,' he said. 'Albot is programmed to calculate meteorological changes.'

'Come again?' said Miss Marbles.

'He can tell you the weather – and he's never wrong,' said Norris.

Dennis Trigg rose from his seat. The weather was his area of expertise after all.

'Let's start with something simple – what will the weather be at 2.35 p.m. precisely?' he asked.

Stan glanced at the clock which stood at
2.30 p.m. Norris repeated the question. Albot
whirred as lights blinked on and off in his head.
He spoke in a harsh, electronic voice.

WEATHER
FOR 2.35 P.M.
11 JUNE
RAINFALL...
HEAVY...

Stan looked out of the window. Outside,
the sky was a brilliant blue and rainfall seemed
about as likely as a plague of frogs. There was a
long silence while everyone waited expectantly.
Nothing happened, apart from Norris losing
his smug smile. Miss Marbles stepped forward
and spoke.

'Well, thank you, Norris, a talking robot is very clever but it's probably wiser to leave weather forecasting to …'

RUMBLE, RUMBLE …

Her words were drowned out by a deafening roll of thunder. Seconds later, rain fell hammering against the window like giant hailstones.

As quickly as it had started, the rain stopped. Stan glanced at the hall clock – the downpour had happened at precisely 2.35 p.m.

Dennis Trigg had turned pale.

'But that's … that's impossible,' he stammered.

'Told you,' said Norris triumphantly. 'Albot is never wrong, and that's only a fraction of what he can do.'

'Thank you, I think that will do for now,' said Miss Marbles. She announced that the judges would retire for a few minutes to decide on the winner. Stan looked at Miles and Minnie.

'That was insane!' he said. 'How did Norris do it?'

Miles shrugged. 'It's obviously a trick,' he said. 'He probably looked up the weather forecast beforehand.'

'Even so, the rain started right on time,' said Minnie.

'If it was rain,' said Miles. 'Maybe someone's on the roof emptying buckets of water?'

It didn't seem likely. When Stan really
thought about it, the only explanation he could
see was that Norris's pet robot had done what
he claimed. But that was impossible. No one
could predict the weather to the exact minute.

Miss Marbles and Dennis Trigg were back
on stage. In his hands, Dennis held the Science
Award Trophy.

'I am proud to announce the winner of the
Dame Dorothy Wingnut Prize for Science,' he

said. 'This year the award goes to … Norris Trimble.'

Miles let out a groan of disappointment.

'Never mind. At least you came close,' said Minnie.

Miles shook his head. 'A tinpot robot that predicts the weather?' he said. 'I mean, it's hardly going to change the world, is it?'

'Probably not,' agreed Stan, although as he spoke he scratched his right ear. He'd earned his nickname Dangerboy because his ears tingled whenever danger was in the air. Worryingly, they were tingling right now.

Chapter 4
Heads You Lose

Later that afternoon, Norris Trimble wheeled Albot down the corridor. In his pocket he had the book token he'd got for winning the Science Prize and he was wondering how to spend it. Maybe on *101 Science Projects for Junior Geniuses*, a book he'd had his eye on for some time. As he passed the science lab, he noticed someone had left a light on.

'Hello? Anyone here?' he called out. The next thing he knew someone grabbed him, pulled him inside and slammed the door shut.

He was shoved roughly into a chair and found a desk lamp shining in his eyes. A figure stepped out in front of him.

'Mr Trigg!' gasped Norris.

'Hello, Norris,' smiled Dennis Trigg. 'I thought we'd have a quiet little chat, just you and me.'

'But I'm supposed to be back in lessons,' protested Norris.

'Don't worry, this won't take long,' said Trigg. 'So tell me, how did you do it?'

'Do what?' asked Norris.

'Don't give me that, the trick with the rain,' snapped Trigg.

'It wasn't a trick,' said Norris.

Trigg's small moustache twitched with impatience. He leaned in closer. Norris could smell egg on his breath.

'You're telling me that your robot can predict the weather, to the exact second?' he said.

'Well, no, not predict,' admitted Norris. 'As any fool knows, weather forecasting isn't an exact science. I decided to take out the uncertainty by programming Albot to change the weather.'

Trigg's eyes narrowed.

'Change? You don't mean … control it?' he frowned.

'Yes, exactly,' said Norris. He wondered what Trigg was after – possibly his book token. The TV weatherman had a wild look in his eye.

'This is incredible,' said Trigg. 'Explain, boy. How does it work?'

Norris sat forward. 'Well, first I installed a D4 hypersonic transmitter…'

'Yes, yes, spare me the technical drivel,' interrupted Trigg. 'I mean what does it DO?'

'Well, the transmitter sends a signal into the atmosphere,' explained Norris. 'It can alter

the weather any way you like. Rain, ice, snow —
anything at all.'

'A transmitter?' repeated Trigg thoughtfully.
'And that would be inside the head, I suppose?'

He turned to Albot, who was lying
abandoned on the floor. Norris watched
uneasily as Trigg used a screwdriver to remove
the robot's helmet-shaped head.

Next he did something even more alarming. He fitted the robot's helmet over his head so that he resembled a weird half-human android.

'How do I activate it?' he said in a muffled voice.

'Don't do that,' said Norris. 'I mean, it's not safe …'

'Let me be the judge of that,' snapped Trigg. 'I've waited all my life for something like this. To actually control the weather – that's power beyond my dreams. I'm not going to miss out because you think it's not safe!'

'Don't do it!' begged Norris. 'You don't know what …'

But his words were drowned out. Trigg had found the ON switch and pressed it. There was a loud buzz and the crackle of thousands of volts of electricity surging into the robot's helmet.

For a second, Trigg lit up like a giant
Catherine wheel before collapsing on the floor.
He lay still, while blue sparks fizzed and died in
the air.

'Mr Trigg?' whispered Norris. 'Are you all
right?'

Trigg's foot twitched, then his fingers
slowly uncurled. Unsteadily, he rose to his feet
and his robotic head swivelled round. Norris
stared. Something terrible had happened!
He could no longer tell whether the creature
before him was Albot or Dennis Trigg, because
they'd merged to become one. The violent
power surge had created some sort of evil
robot creature (which is one good reason why
you should never play with electricity).

Norris backed towards the door.

'Wait there, Mr Trigg, I'll fetch Miss
Marbles,' he stammered.

'SILENCE, WEAKLING!' roared
the creature, in a voice that echoed round

the laboratory. '**I AM THUNDERBOT, LORD OF WEATHER!**'

The evil robot crossed to the window and pointed a finger to the skies. Immediately there came an answering roll of thunder. Norris dived under a desk and hid his head.

'HEH! HEH! HEH!' cackled
Thunderbot. Norris crawled on his belly
towards the door, trying to escape. But a hand
snaked out, picking him up by one foot.

'Please … I won't tell on you!' yelped
Norris. 'Let me go!'

The robot dangled him upside down like a
helpless mouse.

'You're in luck, Norris,' it buzzed. 'Every evil mastermind needs an assistant – someone to carry out menial tasks like shopping and checking batteries. So I am going to give you a simple choice: join me – ᑌᖇ DIE!'

erm...can I think about it?

Chapter 5

A Touch of Wind

Meanwhile, Stan and his friends had changed into their sports kit and arrived at the gym for their Friday PT lesson. This morning there was no sign of their usual teacher, old Mr Weevil. In his place was a battleship in jogging bottoms.

'Good morning, my name is Miss Bulstrode,' she said. 'Mr Weevil is off sick so I'm your new PT instructor.'

Stan exchanged worried looks with Miles.

Miss Bulstrode looked like she meant business. Her navy blue tracksuit was stretched tight across her broad shoulders and her hair was scraped back in a bun.

'PT,' she said. 'Who can tell me what that stands for?'

Miles raised his hand. 'Playtime?'

'Wrong, physical training,' barked Miss Bulstrode. 'Miss Marbles tells me that you're here because of your exceptional talents. Well, excuse me if I'm not impressed. Only one thing interests me – your fitness and stamina.'

'Isn't that two things?' asked Minnie.

'QUIET!' boomed Miss Bulstrode. 'Ten press-ups, NOW!'

As Minnie got down on the floor, Stan wondered if he might be excused for the good of his health. Miss Bulstrode warned them she would not tolerate shirkers or skivers in her class.

Miles nudged Stan. 'Where's Norris?' he whispered.

Stan shrugged. 'Don't ask me, maybe he's late.'

'YOU!' bellowed the teacher, making them jump. 'Yes, the boy at the back! Are you talking while I'm talking?'

Stan turned red. Everyone turned round to stare at him.

'Out here,' ordered Miss Bulstrode. Stan trailed out to the front. His ears started to prickle, which only made him more nervous – though facing Miss Bulstrode was enough to make anyone nervous. She resembled an angry rhino that might charge at any moment.

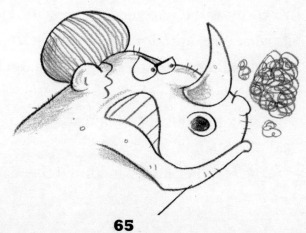

'Name?' she demanded.

'Stan.'

'Well, Stan, you think you're already a superhero? That you've got nothing left to learn?' said the teacher. Stan shook his head dumbly.

'Speak up, boy!'

'No, miss,' mumbled Stan.

He caught sight of his friends' worried faces. Behind them, Tank, the class bully, was enjoying every moment of this.

'So let's find out what you're made of,' said Miss Bulstrode.

She disappeared into the gym cupboard and returned with a set of weights. Stan watched anxiously as she selected two weights the size of truck tyres and threaded them on to a metal bar. Miss Bulstrode stood over the barbell and rolled her shoulders back.

'Strength, effort and determination,' she said. 'Watch me.'

She bent her knees and lifted the massive

barbell on to her chest as if it was a lolly stick. With her muscles bulging, she raised it above her head. The class clapped as she lowered the weight easily to the floor and let it drop with a clang.

'Nothing to it,' she said. 'Right then, Stan, you have a go.'

Stan swallowed. 'Me?' he said. He might as well try to lift a double decker bus! Miss Bulstrode folded her arms.

'Well? Don't keep me waiting,' she said.

Stan looked at the barbell. He wasn't known for his strength; he was much better at knowing when to run away. In fact, now seemed like a good moment.

He bent over the barbell, gripping it with both hands.

'Back straight, bend your knees and LIFT!' barked Miss Bulstrode.

Stan breathed hard, screwed his eyes shut and heaved. The weight didn't budge off the floor. Tank hooted with laughter.

'QUIET!' snapped Miss Bulstrode. 'Put some effort into it, boy! Are you a quitter?'

Stan's cheeks flushed. He breathed hard, gripped the bar once more and heaved.

This time he got it off the ground up until it was level with his knees. But his legs were shaking and starting to buckle under the weight.

'UP, UP, UP!' yelled Miss Bulstrode.

Stan got the barbell on to his chest, but the weight was tipping him backwards. His legs had turned to jelly. Out of the corner of his eye he caught sight of a face at the window. It was Norris Trimble, who was trying to mouth something: 'Hello!' or possibly 'HEEEEELP!'

Stan's legs folded like a deck chair and he crashed back to the floor. The weight fell on his chest, pinning him to the ground. Grinning faces appeared above him. Miss Bulstrode lifted the barbell and hauled him up by one hand. Then she thumped him hard on the back, knocking the breath out of him.

'HOPELESS!' she barked. 'But full marks for effort. Give me a few terms and I'll make a man of you yet!'

Stan doubted if he could last a few terms of Miss Bulstrode, but right now he had other things to worry about. He pointed to the window but was too out of breath to speak.

'Nice going, Stan,' said Miles. 'You should enter the Olympics.'

'NORRIS!' Stan blurted out at last, finding his voice. 'He was at the window!'

They turned, just in time to catch sight of two figures stumbling away across the school field towards the gates. The tall one with the giant head seemed to be dragging Norris along by the arm. Pudding, who had been waiting outside the gym, began barking excitedly.

'Where's he going?' asked Minnie.

'I don't know,' replied Stan. 'I think he needs help.'

There was no time to explain the situation to Miss Bulstrode. If they weren't quick, the two figures would reach the gates and be out of sight. This was a job for **the Invincibles**.

They burst out of the door and on to the field. Norris was fifty metres ahead and looked back over his shoulder.

'HELP!' he cried. 'Kidnap! Robbery! Murder!'

Stan thought he should make up his mind but it was clear Norris was in trouble. The tall figure who had hold of him suddenly whipped round to face them. Stan let out a gasp. The creature had a man's body but the head of a robot. It looked like Norris's science project had come to life and taken him prisoner.

'**FOOLS! IMBECILES!**' cried the mad robot. 'You dare to challenge the mighty **THUNDERBOT**?'

'Thunderbot?' repeated Stan. 'Who on earth is that?'

Minnie took a step forward.

'That's our friend you've got there,' she said.

'Well, he's hardly a friend,' objected Miles.

The evil robot pushed Norris roughly aside. His head swivelled and his eyes flashed like warning lights. '**STAY BACK!**' he ordered them.

'Oh yeah? Make me, tinhead!' Minnie shouted back.

Stan had a feeling she shouldn't have said that. The robot looked up and pointed to the heavens. Immediately the sky began to turn ominously dark. Stan looked up.

'I don't want to worry you, but maybe we should get inside,' he said.

'Don't be such a wimp,' scoffed Minnie. 'It's only a spot of rain!'

But it wasn't rain at all. The air grew heavy and the clouds began to mass like dark boulders. Suddenly Stan saw it coming their way — a black twisting corkscrew beyond the road, growing bigger and bigger.

'TORNADO!' gasped Miles.

Minnie stared. 'You've got to be kidding! We don't get tornadoes,' she said.

'We do now!' said Stan. 'RUN!'

They turned and raced for cover. The tornado roared, whipping across the field and lifting a set of goalposts off the ground. The next moment it hit them …

Chapter 6

Happy Landings

Stan fell out of the sky.

Luckily for him, he landed on something soft – which turned out to be Mrs Sponge's compost heap, where the school dinner slops were emptied.

The Invincibles picked themselves up, brushing bits of egg and carrot from their costumes. Stan picked a blob of mashed potato out of his hair. He smelt of rotten vegetables.

'YUCK!' he said.

'At least we're alive,' said Minnie. 'Not many people survive a tornado.'

Stan looked back over the school field. The tornado had passed over, leaving a trail of destruction on the field. Fences lay flattened and it didn't look like they'd be using the mangled goalposts for a while. In the mayhem Norris and his robot captor had disappeared. The question was, where did Thunderbot's amazing powers come from?

Stan squelched to the door and opened it. Unfortunately he had forgotten about their class teacher.

'And where do you think you're going?' barked Miss Bulstrode.

'Um … to get changed?' said Stan.

The teacher folded her brawny arms.

'First you'll report to the head teacher and explain why you left my class without asking.'

'But we had to …' began Minnie.

'Don't answer back!' stormed Miss Bulstrode. 'And you can clear up all this mess too. It looks like a hurricane came this way.'

Miles was about to say that actually it was a tornado but a look from Minnie silenced him. They splodged past their classmates, who all stood aside to let them pass.

Ten minutes later, Stan and his friends stood in Miss Marbles' study, trying to explain what had happened.

'A tornado?' said Miss Marbles.

'Yes,' said Stan. 'It was massive — you must have seen it!'

'I had the blinds down,' said Miss Marbles. 'And what caused this tornado?'

'An evil robot!' answered Miles. 'Or at least a man with a robot's head.'

'He calls himself Thunderbot,' added Minnie.

Miss Marbles set down her mug of tea.

'Really,' she sighed. 'Every time I turn my back this school seems to be threatened by aliens or lunatic robots. And you say Norris has something to do with all this?'

Stan nodded. 'It's his robot, but it seems to have taken him prisoner,' he said.

'Well, I'm sure there's a reasonable explanation,' said Miss Marbles. 'Knowing Norris, it's probably some sort of scientific experiment.'

'I'm not so sure,' said Stan. 'At least come to the science lab with us – that's where he kept Albot.'

Miss Marbles stood up. 'Very well,' she said. 'But I hope this isn't wasting my time.'

They made their way to the science lab, where the door was open and there were signs of some sort of struggle. Albot lay sprawled on the floor – or at least what was left of him, since he'd completely lost his head. A chair lay on its side while a strange burning smell hung in the air.

'See?' said Minnie. 'Norris has gone and his robot's in pieces.'

Stan stared at Albot's headless body. He'd just remembered something – Thunderbot had been wearing funny clothes: a grey suit that badly needed ironing and a terrible tie. Only one person he knew dressed that badly …

'Dennis Trigg!' cried Stan. 'It's him!'

'What is?' said Miss Marbles.

'The thing that took Norris,' said Stan. 'It was Dennis Trigg! He's somehow become an evil robot with superpowers.'

Miss Marbles frowned. 'Is that even possible?' she said.

'Well, yes! It happens in comic books all the time,' answered Miles.

Minnie looked worried.

'And this robot Dennis, he can actually change the weather?' she said.

'Not just change it,' said Stan. 'From what I saw, he can make it do anything he likes. Who knows what he might do next!'

Miss Marbles tidied Albot's body away into a cupboard.

'Well, I'm sure there's no need to worry,' she said. 'Dennis Trigg is a perfectly sensible man, I can't imagine he'd do anything silly.'

Chapter 7
Eggy

Meanwhile, in a cheap cafe across town, the evil Thunderbot was planning his next move over egg and chips with a mug of strong tea. Seated opposite him, Norris was aware of the other customers' stares. It was most likely because his companion looked like Frankenstein's monster and drinking tea was causing blue sparks to come out of his head.

'It's not fair,' grumbled Norris. 'How come you get chips and I don't?'

'Because I am a WEATHER LORD and you are a worthless slave,' snapped Thunderbot. 'And I've told you before to address me as "LORD AND MASTER".'

Norris bit into his digestive biscuit. 'So, what now?' he asked.

'What now, LORD AND MASTER?'

'OK, what now, Lord and Master?' sighed Norris.

'We lie low while I think of a master plan,' said Thunderbot. 'I'm going to teach my enemies a lesson.'

'What enemies?' asked Norris.

'All those brainless morons that called me boring,' replied Thunderbot. 'My bosses, the TV critics, the so-called experts, the journalists, people who watch television ...'

My old boss

My ENemies

TV critic

Noisy Neighbours

ONe direction

Traffic Wardens

Meddling Kids

'Right,' said Norris. It sounded like a pretty long list of enemies. 'But what can you do? I mean they're not going to give you your job back now that you ... well ...'

'Look like a robot?' said Thunderbot. 'You're mistaken; I don't want my job back. Who wants to be a mere weather forecaster? No, from now on I'm going to make the weather. And believe me, by the time I'm finished they'll be begging me to stop!'

He brought his fist down on his plate, sending chips flying in all directions. Norris quickly gobbled one up.

'But it's only the weather,' he said. 'I mean, a bit of rain isn't going to scare anyone.'

'What a feeble imagination you have,' sneered Thunderbot.

His eyes flicked to the TV screen on the opposite wall, which was showing the national weather forecast. The smiling weather reporter stood in front

of a map, pointing to bright blobs of sunshine dotting the country.

Thunderbot made a noise like a printer with a paper jam. It took Norris a moment to realise he was laughing.

'HEH! HEH! HEH! Sunny spells, is it?' he sniggered. 'We'll see about that!'

He crossed to the cafe's dirty window and looked up at the sky.

'What are you doing?' asked Norris.

The other customers were staring again. Most people didn't leave their chips to get cold, but then most people didn't have robot heads with blazing eyes. Thunderbot looked back at Norris, then pointed a finger at the sky.

In seconds, clouds rolled in from nowhere, blotting out the sun. Passers-by looked up, startled, children stopped playing and cats scuttled under cars. White flakes had started to fall.

'It's snowing!' shouted Norris. People rushed to the window to join him.

'It can't be! It's summer!' they cried.

'It is! Look!'

Outside, the snow was falling fast, carpeting the streets. Cars skidded on the road and children ran up and down whooping with excitement. In less than a minute the snow lay so deep that it reached people's knees and made their summer shorts look faintly ridiculous.

Thunderbot turned back to the TV screen, where the weather reporter was still predicting glorious sunny weather.

'You see, fools?' cried Thunderbot. 'And this is just the beginning. Soon I will bring chaos to the country and no one will dare to stand in my way! Then I will RULE THE WORLD!'

Chapter 8
Summer Craze

Miss Marbles switched off the TV and turned to **the Invincibles**. They were among the small handful of children – and one dog – that had made it into school despite the arctic weather. They sat in the head teacher's office wearing hats and scarves and drinking hot chocolate.

'Well?' said Miss Marbles. 'What do you make of it?'

'That's him all right,' replied Minnie. 'Dennis Trigg.'

'Except now he's a crackpot evil robot,'
said Miles.

Miss Marbles shook her head – evil robots
were the worst. She blamed herself for not
keeping a closer eye on what Norris was up to
in the science lab. Who would have thought that
nice Dennis Trigg could turn out to be a maniac
who'd threaten the nation?

The snow had been falling for three days and nights. Miss Marbles had only managed to reach school on a pair of skis that she hadn't used since she was nineteen.

She took off her glasses and rubbed her eyes. 'But why take Norris?' she asked. 'What does he want with him?'

'Don't forget it was Norris who made Albot,' Stan pointed out. 'He might be useful.'

'In any case we don't have much time,' Minnie reminded them. 'The message said he'll strike at noon tomorrow.'

'Unless the government pays up,' said Stan. Miss Marbles shook her head.

'One trillion pounds?' she said. 'I can't even count that much.'

'I can,' claimed Miles. 'One trillion is one thousand billion so if you multiply …'

'Yes, Miles, we get the picture,' said Stan.

'The heart of the nation,' Miss Marbles repeated to herself. 'What does that mean?'

Stan shrugged. He'd never been very good at solving riddles.

'Surely London's the heart of the nation?' said Miles. 'Isn't it the capital?'

'Yes, but London's a very big place,' said Miss Marbles.

They all fell silent, trying to think.

'Perhaps he's going to attack the Houses of Parliament?' suggested Minnie.

'Or the Prime Minister?' said Stan. 'He said the "beating heart", so maybe it's a person.'

Minnie shot out of her seat. 'The QUEEN!' she cried.

'She's the beating heart of the nation. He's going to attack the queen!'

Stan's ears began to throb in alarm. If Minnie was right, then tomorrow Thunderbot would launch some kind of attack on Buckingham Palace. The queen might be in terrible danger and they were the only ones who knew it.

'But this is dreadful!' said Miss Marbles. 'Good gracious, the queen! We have to do something!'

'Shouldn't we tell the police?' asked Miles.

'I very much doubt they'll listen,' said Miss Marbles. 'Besides, they'll say that Buckingham Palace is guarded day and night. No, someone must protect the queen and it has to be you.'

'US?' said Stan. 'What can we do? London's miles away!

'And the roads will be impossible!' added Minnie.

Miles looked out of the window at the school bus, half buried in snow.

'Miss Marbles,' he said. 'Can we borrow your skis a minute? I've got an idea.'

Booster Jets

snow plough made from school gates

Skis under wheels

DON'T BE GOOD, BE SUPER.

PROPERTY OF MIGHTY HIGH SCHOOL

The Pocket Guide for Superheroes

Everything you need to know
to save the world.

9
EVIL ULTIMATUMS

Ask yourself, what do super-criminals want? World domination, naturally. Generally they start out small, say by stealing lunchboxes from little kids. But given time they will graduate to stealing deadly missiles or poisoning the oceans. At this point you can be pretty sure they will issue AN EVIL ULTIMATUM. Typically it goes like this:

DR. NOGOOD

B.A. M.A. N.A.S.T.Y.

YOUR FRIENDLY LOCAL SUPER CRIMINAL

Dear Sir,
You have until dawn/midnight/
I get bored of waiting...to
hand over the gold/cash/
presidency...or else I will
activate the bomb/destroy
planet earth/ do something
so unspeakably evil that
I can't speak of it.

Regards

Dr Nogood

Dr Nogood.

If you find yourself faced with an EVIL ULTIMATUM you have three choices:

A) Ignore it

B) Give in

C) Find your enemy before the deadline is up

A) is risky and B) expensive so C) is obviously your best option. In this case, you don't have much time so why are you wasting precious minutes reading this book?

Stay calm; remember no EVIL ULTIMATUM has ever resulted in the destruction of the earth – although there's always a first time.

Chapter 10
Doomsday

The next morning the school bus finally reached London. It had been a long, hazardous journey, especially since Miss Marbles was wearing her reading glasses to drive. **The Invincibles** spilled out of the bus and waited for their legs to stop trembling.

They looked around. The streets of London were eerily silent and empty of traffic. Snow lay on the ground as thick and cold as school rice pudding. The fountain in the square looked like a giant wedding cake hung with icicles.

A few people were about, but most were police on duty because the city was on full alert. Stan shivered. Miles had brought his Mega Gloves, insisting that they would come in useful.

'Excuse me, madam, is that your bus?' asked a police sergeant. 'I'm afraid you can't leave it there.'

Miss Marbles took off her glasses. 'Sergeant, we've driven a very long way and we don't have much time,' she said.

'Maybe not, but you can't park there,' insisted the policeman.

Minnie tried to explain. 'Please, this is an emergency,' she said. 'The queen could be in danger!'

The sergeant eyed their bright blue costumes and red capes. 'I'm sorry, I didn't recognise you,' he said dryly. 'You'd be superheroes, I suppose?'

'That's right,' said Minnie. 'We're **the Invincibles**. I'm Frisbee Girl, this is Dangerboy and Brainiac.'

'And I'm Batman,' said the policeman. 'But you'll still have to move the bus.'

Minnie was about to argue but Miss Marbles shook her head. They left her to deal with the policeman, while they set off in search of Buckingham Palace. They hurried through the snowbound streets, passing police on every corner.

'Is this the right way? What's her house look like?' asked Miles.

'Probably something like that,' said Minnie, pointing ahead.

At the end of the road was an enormous white palace. A royal standard fluttered in the courtyard, indicating that the queen was at home. The palace was protected by tall iron gates with soldiers in red uniforms standing on guard.

'Wow!' said Miles. 'The queen lives there?'

'Last time I heard,' said Minnie. 'Come on, we've got to get in.'

It wasn't going to be easy, especially as the two guards didn't seem to want to talk.

'We need to see the queen,' Minnie told them.

'Urgently,' added Stan. 'It's a matter of life and death – and bad weather.'

The guards stood like statues, staring straight ahead.

'This is hopeless,' sighed Stan. 'We'll never get in!'

Just then, Pudding spotted a fat pigeon in the palace courtyard and wriggled under the gates to give chase.

'HEY! STOP!' cried one of the guards, springing to life.

Within seconds, both the guards had left their posts and were chasing Pudding across the courtyard, trying to catch him. Stan looked at Minnie.

'I guess we can go in, then,' he said.

With no one to stop them, they slipped through the front gates.

'What now?' asked Miles, looking up at the great palace. 'Do we ring the doorbell and ask for the queen?'

But Stan wasn't listening, because his ears were suddenly on full alert. Snow whipped into

the air as the wind picked
up. Pudding came running
back to Minnie and
barked.

'It's starting!' cried
Stan. 'Better take cover!'

They looked around,
but the courtyard didn't offer
any shelter apart from the tall
flagpole. Now the wind was beginning to
roar. Stan raised an arm, half blinded by snow.
Miles was struggling with his gloves.

'Hang on to me!' he yelled.

'What for?' shouted Stan.

'Don't argue, just do it!'

They leaned against the gale. Stan grabbed
Miles round the waist while Minnie held on to
Stan with one hand and Pudding with the other.
Miles's magnetic gloves clamped him to the
metal flagpole. They hung on for dear life as the
storm struck, lifting them off their feet.

Trees bent in the gale, police cars were swept down the road like leaves and a soldier's black busby shot past them at high speed. Stan shut his eyes and held on grimly to Miles. Then, as suddenly as it had begun, the storm passed over and the wind died away.

The Invincibles fell to earth with a thud.

'That wasn't so bad,' gasped Miles. 'I think we're safe now.'

'SORRY TO DISAPPOINT YOU,' said a voice.

Stan looked up. A menacing figure wearing a bad suit stood in the courtyard. Thunderbot had arrived.

Chapter 11

Battle Royal

The Invincibles got shakily to their feet. Pudding the Wonderdog whimpered and ran to hide behind Minnie's legs.

'So, what have we here?' said Thunderbot. 'School friends of yours, Norris?'

Norris pulled a face. 'Not really,' he sneered. 'They call themselves **the Invincibles** but actually they're pretty useless.'

'Oh yeah?' said Stan. 'At least we're on the right side. What's your excuse, Norris?'

Norris shrugged. It wasn't his fault if he'd
created an Evil Robot who was trying to take
over the world. It could have happened to
anyone.

Minnie drew her frisbee from her belt.

'The game's up,' she said. 'You won't get
near the queen. The streets are swarming
with police.'

'Really?' The robot's head swivelled round. 'Funny, but I don't see them anywhere,' he said.

Beyond the gates Stan saw that the streets were deserted. The hurricane had swept everything away. All that remained was a police car lodged in the branches of a tree. If there was going to be a fight, they were on their own.

'Run along, kiddies,' said Thunderbot. 'This is your last warning.'

'Better do as he says,' nodded Norris.

Minnie had other ideas. Suddenly her
frisbee went skimming through the air
and struck the robot right
between the eyes.

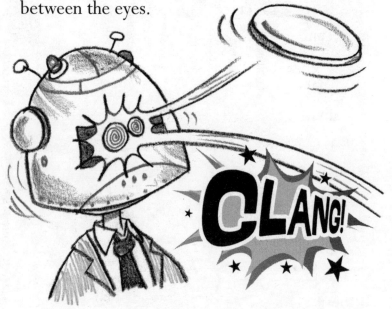

The robot shook his head as if a fly had just
landed on him.

'You shouldn't have done that,' he said.
'And now I think it's my turn.'

Stan's ears began to burn. He had a very
bad feeling about this.

RAIN FELL IN TORRENTS

HAILSTONES AS BIG AS FOOTBALLS LASHED THEM

THE TEMPERATURE DROPPED TO THIRTY BELOW ZERO AS A FIERCE ICE STORM BLEW IN FROM THE NORTH

WHEN IT PASSED...

'Ready to give in?' demanded Thunderbot.

Stan spoke through chattering teeth. 'N– …
n– … never.'

'You are wasting my time,' snorted the
robot. 'I didn't come here to play games. Where
is the queen?'

'You missed her,' replied Minnie. 'She's out
er … walking the dogs.'

'Do you take me for a fool?' snapped
Thunderbot. 'She's in there, hiding, but it won't
save her.'

'You wouldn't hurt the queen,' said Stan.

'Wouldn't I?' replied Thunderbot. 'You
forget, I'm not a weak-willed human like
you. Tell me, have you ever seen a lightning
storm?'

'No,' said Minnie.

'What is it they say? "You never know
where lightning will strike",' said Thunderbot,
his eyes glinting. 'Whole buildings can burst
into flames, even royal palaces.'

Stan looked up at the windows of
Buckingham Palace. The queen was in there
somewhere and she was in danger. They had
to do something – but what? If only they
could erect a force field around the palace but
all they had was Miles' magnetic gloves. Some
help they were in a lightning storm! Wait a
minute, thought Stan. He dimly remembered
something he'd learned in a science lesson. It
was their only chance.

'Miles,' he said
in a loud whisper.
'Don't let him have
the gloves!'

'Gloves?'
Thunderbot's head
swivelled round to
face them.

Miles hid the
Mega Gloves behind
his back, but too late.

'Give them to me!' snapped Thunderbot, holding out his hand. 'Ah yes, these gloves. Remind me, what do they do?'

'All kinds of things,' said Stan, thinking quickly. 'For instance, whoever wears them is protected from danger.'

'Are they?' frowned Miles. It was certainly news to him. What in Zog's name was Stan playing at? Anyone would think he wanted the robot to have the gloves.

'Then I will keep them,' said Thunderbot, trying them on. 'Now, where was I?'

'The lightning storm,' Stan reminded him.

'Of course,' said Thunderbot. 'They used to call me boring – boring Dennis Trigg, well how's this for boring, hmm? Stand by for fireworks!'

'But, master …' began Norris.

'Silence, fool!' snarled Thunderbot. He pointed to the heavens and instantly was answered by a low rumble of thunder. Pudding yelped and hid his eyes with his paws. Seconds later the first bolt of lightning lit up the sky.

'HEH! HEH! HEH!' cackled the Evil Robot, taking a step back to enjoy the show. 'Just one step closer,' muttered Stan.

Stan, Minnie and Miles gathered round. Without his shattered robot helmet, Dennis Trigg looked as harmless as a pet hamster, though slightly burnt at the edges.

'I learnt that in science,' said Stan. 'Never stand under a tree in a lightning storm – or a flagpole, for that matter.'

A siren wailed in the distance, growing louder. As they stood waiting for the police to arrive, a small gate behind them creaked open. A grey-haired woman wearing a blue coat and a silver tiara stepped into the palace grounds, herding a bunch of excited corgis. She stopped to give them a little wave before disappearing through a door into the palace.

The Invincibles stood for a moment, lost for words.

'Was that … who I think it was?' asked Minnie.

Stan nodded. 'And to think, she was out walking the dogs all the time!'

Chapter 12

One is Thanked

The following Monday, Stan and his friends were called into Miss Marbles' office. Outside, the sky was a perfect blue. Warm summer days had returned after the fog, ice and blizzards that had been playing havoc with the weather forecasts.

'Well,' said Miss Marbles. 'It was a close thing, but thanks to you the country is safe and no one came to any harm.'

'Well, apart from Dennis Trigg,' Stan pointed out. 'Is he going to be OK?'

'Still in hospital, I gather,' said Miss Marbles.
'I'm sure his eyebrows will grow back in time.
He claims he doesn't remember anything at all.'

'Norris was partly to blame,' said Minnie.
'Something happened when Dennis put on that
robot helmet. He became power mad.'

'I agree with you, Minnie,' said Miss
Marbles. 'And I've warned Norris that there'll
be no more robots from now on. If he wants

to experiment, he can help Mrs Sponge in the kitchen.'

Stan raised his eyebrows. Norris helping in the kitchen? School dinners were bad enough as it was!

'Was that why you wanted to see us?' asked Minnie.

'Oh no, I was forgetting,' said Miss Marbles. 'A letter arrived for you this morning.'

She handed it over. Minnie stared at the envelope, which bore a royal coat of arms.

'I think it's from Buckingham Palace,' said Miss Marbles.

Minnie tore open the envelope and took out the letter. The others gathered round.

HRH THE QUEEN
Flat 2, Buckingham Palace, London

Dear Children,

It has been bought to my attention that I owe you a word of thanks. I gather that a certain individual calling himself Thunderbox (or something of the sort) broke into the palace grounds and made nasty threats. I gather that this same person is responsible for the dreadful weather, which has ruined my strawberry beds. I am very fond of strawberries but I will not put up with nasty threats. The police inform me that you showed great bravery to bring this criminal to justice. So this letter comes with my sincere thanks.

Next time you are in London, please do drop by to look around the palace with no charge.

Mrs Queen

Her Royal Highness, the Queen

PS You owe me £75.50 for the repair of one flagpole.

Stan stared. 'The queen!' he said. 'The queen wrote to us!'

'Only because she wants a new flagpole,' Miles pointed out.

'Don't be silly,' said Miss Marbles. 'It isn't everyone who gets a personal letter of thanks from the queen – you should all be very proud.'

Stan felt himself grow a little taller. The queen! His mum was never going to believe this!

'By the way, Miles,' said Miss Marbles. 'How's that invention of yours? Magic gloves, wasn't it?'

'Magnetic gloves,' corrected Miles. 'And they probably saved our lives.'

'Really?' said Miss Marbles. 'May I see them?'

Miles produced the shiny gloves and the head teacher tried them on.

'So, what do I do exactly?' she asked.

'Point them at anything metal, but be careful – they're pretty powerful,' warned Miles.

Miss Marbles cast around for a metal object and settled on the chandelier hanging from the ceiling.

'How about that?' she suggested.

Stan looked alarmed. 'Wait,' he said. 'Isn't that a bit …'

LOOK OUT FOR MORE

SUPERHERO SCHOOL

ADVENTURES

LOOK OUT FOR MORE

SuperHero School

ADVENTURES

LOOK OUT FOR MORE

SUPERHERO SCHOOL

ADVENTURES

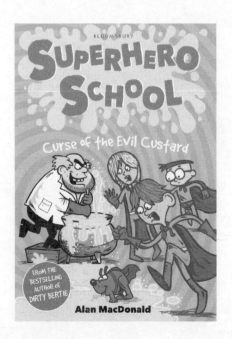